T0198968

Balboa Press books may be ordered through booksellers or by contacting:

Balboa Press
A Division of Hay House
1663 Liberty Drive
Bloomington, IN 47403
www.balboapress.com
844-682-1282

ISBN: 978-1-9822-7949-3 (sc)
ISBN: 978-1-9822-7950-9 (e)

Library of Congress Control Number: 2022902090

Print information available on the last page.

Balboa Press rev. date: 04/22/2022

BALBOA.PRESS
A DIVISION OF HAY HOUSE

It was a gloomy Sunday afternoon as Bruce Wayne rested his chin on the metal frame of the glass kitchen door. The open kitchen door allowed the fresh air to glide pass Bruce Wayne's face as he watched the birds in the backyard, fascinated by the way they flew from branch to branch. He wondered what it felt like to fly like the birds. I bet it's exhilarating, he thought.

Bruce Wayne, his mom and dad had just gotten back from a short hike which Bruce Wayne enjoyed so much. The dampness from the mild rain brought out a variety of smells along the trail that captivated Bruce Wayne and thus, he kept his nose close to the ground. Usually, it would be just him and his mom hiking, so it was a treat to have his dad come along that day. Even though the hike didn't tire him out, the cool, cloudy weather made him feel like a slug.

Maybe he would join his mom and dad when they napped if it continued to drizzle. Napping was a ritual his parents did on Sundays.

From the left corner of the backyard, a slim, dark figure appeared and Bruce Wayne instantly ran towards it knowing who it was....Whoof Whoof!..."Hey Tux!" he greeted happily. "What are you doing out here? I thought cats didn't like getting wet." Tuxford was his cat best friend who had taught him martial arts and also that cats and dogs could be friends.

"We don't, which is why I'm in this raincoat," answered Tuxford. He wore a navy blue, hooded raincoat that covered all his limbs except for his paws.

"So, why are you here?" asked Bruce Wayne again.

"Because I wanted to tell you about the annual race that'll happen in a few weeks!" Tuxford was suddenly animated.

"A race?" Bruce Wayne asked.

"Yes! It happens every year. It encourages the new dogs in the neighborhood to enter the race. It's only a mile they have to run. The new dogs run with other dogs who have lived in the neighborhood for over a year. It's a way for every dog to meet each other," Tux paused for a second, then blurted with excitement "I want you to run this year BW!"

"Huh?" Bruce Wayne was surprised. He enjoyed running with his mom but he never ran against anyone.

"Listen, it's a friendly race, AND there's a pot of GOODIES for the winner," Tux said emphasizing the goodies.

"Oooh...a pot of GOODIES," Bruce Wayne said slowly as his eyes widened at the thought.

Then, out of curiosity he asked, "Why don't you run?"

"Because it's for dogs. Besides, we cats don't like to run as much as you guys. We have our own way of getting to know each other," said Tuxford.

"And what's that?" asked Bruce Wayne.

"Oh, we have a boxing contest. We cats like to use our front paws to smack things around so boxing was a logical choice," said Tuxford matter-of-factly. "We wear boxing gloves to look professional. But nobody gets hurt of course. It's all for fun like the dog race."

Cats with boxing gloves.....hmmm, I would be curious to see that, thought Bruce Wayne.

"Speaking of boxing, did you ever see that movie Rocky?" Tux saw Bruce Wayne shake his head, "Well, it's a classic boxing movie. You should ask your mom if you can watch it. Anyway, there's this old guy who trains Rocky for his fight. I was thinking that maybe I could be your trainer for the race." He paused, then asked, "Will you run?"

"Uhmm...okay!" said Bruce Wayne with a wide smile.

"Cool! We could start training tomorrow when it's supposed to stop raining. I don't like to get wet," said Tuxford, securing his hood around his face so that the sprinkle of rain wouldn't get on it.

"Why do I need to train if it's a race for fun?" asked Bruce Wayne.

"To increase your chance of getting the pot of goodies, of course. And, in the process of training, we'll have a great time," said Tuxford with a grin.

When Tuxford left, Bruce Wayne cheerfully went inside the house. He eagerly asked his mom and dad if he could watch the movie "Rocky". He explained that he was going to run the annual neighborhood dog race and wanted to see the movie for training purposes. Of course, his parents were thrilled and very supportive of his decision. And, since his mom and dad both loved the movie, they decided to watch it with Bruce Wayne.

Even though Bruce Wayne's mom had to cover his eyes a few times during the boxing scenes in the movie, Bruce Wayne felt inspired. He was impressed by the progress Rocky made with his running, which was the part Bruce Wayne focused on. As he watched the movie, Bruce Wayne moved his forelimbs the way Rocky moved his arms each time Rocky ran in the movie, and raised his forelimbs as Rocky lifted his arms in celebration as he made it up to the top of those steps before his big fight.. A little apprehensive, Bruce Wayne hoped that he wouldn't have to eat raw eggs for breakfast because he really loved the food his mom cooked for him.

It had stopped raining the next day and the sun had pierced through the clouds in the late morning. Tuxford came over wearing a whistle around his neck. He had asked Bruce Wayne to open the back gate to the backyard because he had brought something they were going to use for training. When the back gate opened, Tuxford dragged something that had two wheels. Bruce Wayne had never seen anything like it before.

"What is that?" Bruce Wayne asked with much interest.

"It's a rickshaw," said Tux.

"Rickshaw?" Bruce Wayne thought it was a strange looking chair. "What is it for?"

"Well, one person rides on it while another pulls it...that's where you come in, my friend," said Tux watching Bruce Wayne's face go from curiosity to confusion. "You'll be fine, don't worry. Anyway, my dad got this rickshaw in an auction a long time ago. It's been collecting dust in our garage. I figured we could use it later," said Tuxford. "And, this is a jump rope," he continued, as he took the jump rope out of the rickshaw.

"Ooo, I know what that is," said Bruce Wayne proudly. "I've seen my mom use one. And, Rocky used one too."

"Yes, he did. Good. You probably know how to use it then," said Tux. "So, are you ready to train?" asked Tuxford.

"Yes!" Bruce Wayne couldn't contain his eagerness that he started jumping up and down.

"Easy now. You need to harness that energy into your training BW," said Tuxford laughingly. He then reached into his fur pocket and handed Bruce Wayne a stretchy, material thing.

"Nice," said Bruce Wayne, inspecting the circular material given to him. It felt like a towel. "What is this Tux?"

"It's a headband," said Tux. He noticed that Bruce Wayne still looked puzzled. So he took the headband from Bruce Wayne and put it over his head. But because his head was so much smaller than Bruce Wayne's, it slid down to his neck. "It's supposed to sit on your forehead to absorb your sweat during your workouts," he explained. He removed the headband from his neck and handed it back to Bruce Wayne.

Bruce Wayne took the headband and put it over his head. It felt snug. "This feels weird like my head is constipated. Do I really need this?" asked Bruce Wayne.

"Believe me, you will need it, my friend. You're in for a tough workout," replied Tuxford. "Yippee!" Bruce Wayne found himself jumping up and down again but soon stopped. He loved getting a good workout. Each time his mom worked out, he would try to copy all the moves she did.

Even though his mom told him that exercise was good for his health, he did it more for fun.

For thirty minutes, Bruce Wayne had an intense workout. Tuxford made him do so many sprints that his legs felt like jelly. Bruce Wayne was a natural at jumping rope since he had watched his mom jump rope many times. During the whole training, Tuxford moved alongside with Bruce Wayne, doing the same exercises but with much less intensity. It felt like a game to Bruce Wayne.

At one point, Tuxford shouted as Bruce Wayne was running in place, "What do you want?" "Cookies!" Bruce Wayne shouted back and then smiled trying to catch his breath.

"Why do you want them?" Tuxford demanded.

"They're yummy!" Bruce Wayne yelled back joyfully causing them to laugh uncontrollably for a minute before resuming his training.

Even the birds and squirrels in the backyard got infected with their fun and began encouraging Bruce Wayne with his training, especially Sophie, the sparrow. She flew alongside Bruce Wayne each time he did his sprints. She had a soft spot for him because he had always said good morning to her and was very courteous. She liked that.

After having jumped rope for what seemed like ten thousand times, Tuxford made him do sprints to the back gate and then walking lunges towards the house. Bruce Wayne was so tired he felt numb and feeble-minded. He was aware of only his sweat that had started to pour out of his body. Fortunately, the headband did its job and caught the sweat that would have dribbled down to his eyes without it. The workout was beyond what he expected. Tuxford trained him as hard as that old man did with Rocky, thought Bruce Wayne.

In the middle of his training, Bruce Wayne saw his mom stick her head out of the kitchen door. He had hoped that she would save him from his rigorous training, but instead she had gotten her camera out and had taken a picture of him. He tried a weak smile but couldn't muster one.

"Okay, drink some water and take a rest," said Tuxford. "You're doing fantastic BW." "Awesome BW," said Sophie, brimming with pride.

Thank goodness, Bruce Wayne thought as he guzzled some water down. He felt so relieved that he couldn't help but immediately collapse on the ground and sigh. He was happy despite his fatigue. It felt good to lay down, he thought. The only thing missing was a cookie. He could have fallen asleep but he sensed Tuxford standing over him. He opened one eye and asked, "Is the break over already?"

"You've got a few more minutes," Tuxford said with an amused smile.

Sophie flitted above Bruce Wayne trying to fan him with her wings, which he very much appreciated.

After the break, Bruce Wayne did more sprints, running back and forth from the garage door to the back gate, only stopping when Tuxford blew his whistle to signal he was done.

"Okay, now you get to pull me in that rickshaw I brought over and see how far you can run," said Tux.

Huh?!!...Bruce Wayne forgot about the rickshaw. He didn't know how he was going to run while pulling Tux in it....his legs were spent. The lower half of his body felt like heavy mush, and Bruce Wayne didn't feel like he had much control over them.

Later that night after being able to run only a block with Tux on the rickshaw, Bruce Wayne was eager to go to bed early, even though he napped many times during the day.

"How did you like your first training, sweet boy? Did you have fun?" asked his mom. She had decided to do acupuncture on Bruce Wayne to relieve his weary, achy body before he went to bed that night.

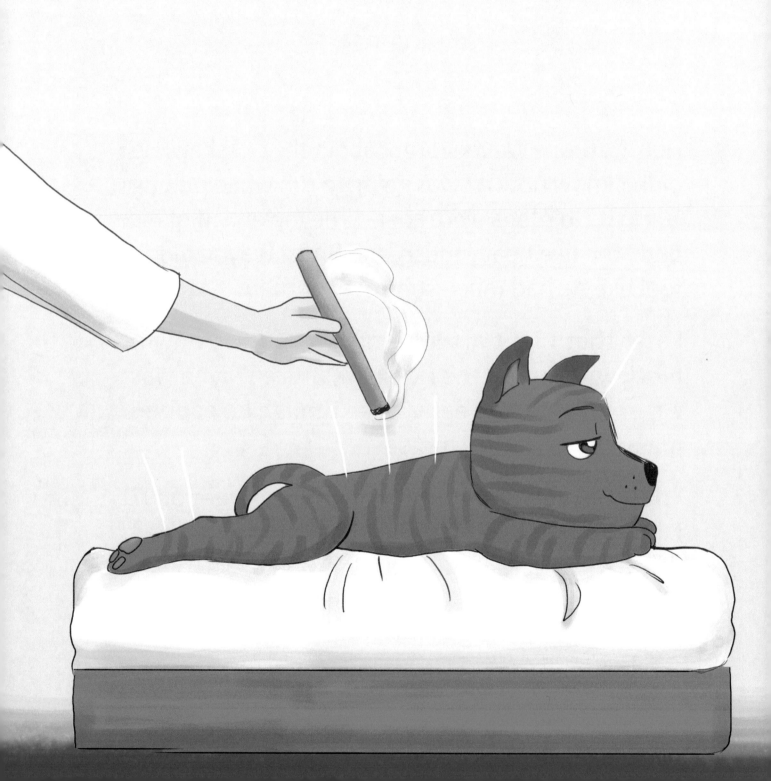

"Yes, I liked it a lot....but I didn't realize that I would get so tired so quickly. It was tougher than I thought it would be," he mumbled. Bruce Wayne felt so good and relaxed from the acupuncture. He took a whiff of the moxa and sighed. He loved the smell of moxa, a black stick that burned at one end, which was the end that his mom waved over the needles. The smell of moxa usually made him feel drowsy and he was close to falling asleep.

"I saw how hard you were working. It looked like a strenuous workout. I thought you were incredible for your first day. Besides, you'll get faster and stronger the more you do it. Just like Rocky did, remember?" said his mom.

"Yeah, Rocky...." he said slowly in a whisper as he fell into slumber.

"Sleep soundly, my sweet boy," his mom said as she kissed his forehead and continued his acupuncture treatment.

As each day passed for the next three weeks of training, Bruce Wayne felt progressively faster, stronger and more agile. He was able to pull Tuxford in the rickshaw comfortably for a few blocks. He felt so cool and proud of himself when he was finally able to put one arm behind his back to do a one-armed push up just like what Rocky did in the movie. He made sure his mom took a picture of that. He felt like Rocky in a pit bull's body. He was certain that he had developed baby muscles on top of his muscles...a thought that made him giggle.

The morning of the race, before Bruce Wayne got out of bed, his mom lovingly embraced him and said, "I want you to know that no matter what happens today, your dad and I think you are already a winner for deciding to run this race and being so dedicated to your training. We just want you to have fun during the race, okay?" Bruce Wayne smiled warmly and nodded.

"One last thing...Make sure you focus on yourself. No one else matters but you," said his mom.

"Okay...but why?" Bruce Wayne was puzzled.

"Because when you pay attention to what other people are doing, you may end up comparing yourself to them, and that's not good. You know why?" asked his mom.

"Why?" Bruce Wayne was very curious.

"Because it prevents you from focusing on what you want to do. It's a distraction, meaning it takes your attention away from what you want. Does that make sense?" asked his mom.

Bruce Wayne listened intently and answered quietly, "I think so." He needed to think about his mom's words a bit more.

Tuxford came over to eat breakfast with Bruce Wayne. Bruce Wayne's mom and dad had left them to be alone. Bruce Wayne ate only one hard-boiled egg for breakfast while Tuxford ate scrambled eggs and a couple of sausages. Bruce Wayne wasn't very hungry since his mom had cooked him a huge bowl of gluten free pasta with beef the night before.

"We have a good hour before the race, so we have time to go over some things," said Tuxford finishing his last breakfast sausage.

"Like what?" asked Bruce Wayne.

"Remembering that the race is for fun, and secondly, keeping your eye on the target," said Tuxford.

"Target? What target?" asked Bruce Wayne.

"The finish line, of course. The first one to reach the finish line will get the pot of goodies," said Tuxford. "Remember, there might be some obstacles during the race."

"I remember. But you don't know what they are," said Bruce Wayne.

"Nope. Last year, there were scattered chew bones along the path of the race, which stopped some dogs from completing the race," said Tuxford.

"Ooh, chew bones are fun," said Bruce Wayne.

"I wouldn't know. So, beware. They may be there again this year," said Tuxford. "If they are, look away."

Look away, Bruce Wayne thought, making a mental note.. "How're you feeling?" Tuxford asked, examining Bruce Wayne. "Invincible!...heehee... that's a new word I learned yesterday," said Bruce Wayne proudly.

For the next half hour, Tuxford purposefully talked about the action movie that he saw recently. They were chatting and laughing so much that they almost forgot the time until Bruce Wayne's mom stuck her head into the kitchen and said that it was time to start heading towards the park.

It was a huge park. When they arrived, they saw at least thirty dogs strolling around socializing. It was a perfect day for running a race. The air was crisp and the clouds covered the sun. Bruce Wayne and Tuxford walked over to the table to check in Bruce Wayne for the race, while Bruce Wayne's parents looked for a place to stand around the race track.

"Welcome to our neighborhood Bruce...," said the old Great Dane sitting behind the table.

"Bruce Wayne, sir," said Bruce Wayne, correcting the Great Dane.

"Excuse me, Bruce Wayne. Please call me Lionel. Here's your tag. Make sure you have it around your neck. The race will start in ten minutes. Best of luck to you," said Lionel.

"Thanks Lionel," said Bruce Wayne as he put on his tag identifying him as number seventeen. He wondered how many dogs were running the race, and suddenly felt nervous. What if he didn't win, he thought. Even though he wanted his mom and dad to see him win, he knew they would be happy no matter what happened. Then he remembered what his mom told him that morning about not comparing himself to anyone and just focusing on what he wanted.

Having fun was the reason he agreed to run the race in the first place, and, of course, the possibility of getting the pot of goodies...yum! But that was an added benefit. Who cares if he won or lost, he was going to have fun....and that instantly made him feel better until.....

He looked at the area assigned for the race and noticed something that made him gasp loudly in disbelief....

"I told you there would be obstacles," said Tuxford, standing beside Bruce Wayne. He saw what caused Bruce Wayne to gasp and recognized the challenge that lay ahead for his best friend.

"Oh no! What are you going to do BW?!" Sophie uttered nervously from above them.

Unbeknownst to Bruce Wayne and Tuxford, she had flown to the park behind them. She was clearly concerned.

"I don't know Sophie," Bruce Wayne said softly. He was flabbergasted. There seemed to be a basket of cookies every one hundred yards along the path of the race. Those weren't obstacles. They were temptations. How could anyone win with those tasty treats, he wondered....run faster?

Alone, Bruce Wayne pensively walked towards the starting line as he heard Tux say, "Focus BW."

Bruce Wayne stood behind the starting line. There were eighteen dogs of different shapes and sizes running the race including himself. Many of the dogs were already drooling at the thought of the baskets ahead of them. He had to wipe his own drool that hung four inches long from the side of his mouth. He couldn't help himself. There were a few dogs that weren't salivating, which he assumed were not food motivated.

There was only a minute left before the race would begin. Bruce Wayne knew he was taking this race too seriously. He remembered something his mom told him a while back, that he can have everything he wanted. He just had to believe he can have it. He took a deep breath and imagined the fun he was going to have running and tasting whatever treats that smelled good to him. He took another deep breath which set his intention and focused. A shot rang, and all the dogs took off running.

Bruce Wayne bolted and felt all his muscles respond amazingly. As he ran, he knew he was focused because he was feeling soooo goooood! As he approached the first basket of cookies, he could smell that they had chicken in them....not his favorite. So he easily ran past the first basket. But he noticed that a number of dogs had stopped to nibble.

Salmon was the flavor in the next basket which Bruce Wayne had no difficulty ignoring. The third basket had beef. The urge was there to stop but it wasn't strong, so Bruce Wayne continued to run. He was now running with five other dogs. The rest had lagged behind lingering around the basket. Lamb was in the fourth basket...eekkthh!!! He recently had tummy problems with lamb...too rich for his belly. He gladly ran past it.

Oohh my....venison....was what Bruce Wayne sniffed in the air two yards away from the fifth basket. He loved venison, and immediately put the brakes on his running along with another dog. But unlike his competitor, as soon as Bruce Wayne grabbed a piece of venison cookie with his mouth, he took off, sucking the cookie like a throat lozenge. From a distance, he heard someone yell, "Run, BW, Run!"......That must have been Tux, thought Bruce Wayne. Delighting in the taste of venison in his mouth, he happily ran faster.

Woohoo!!...I am as fast as a bullet, he thought as he soon caught up with the four dogs who hadn't stopped at any of the baskets.

Fortunately, turkey was the flavor of the sixth basket. Bruce Wayne liked turkey as much as chicken, so he zoomed past it. To his surprise, one of the four dogs decided he couldn't resist turkey, and therefore ran back to the basket.

Minutes passed by and Bruce Wayne saw no sign of a basket. Was that it with the baskets, he wondered. He figured the end of the race was approaching. He noticed that two of the three dogs he was running with were slowing down and starting to drop behind. The other dog, a Doberman Pincher, continued his fast pace. The Doberman Pincher bore a stoic expression on his face that made Bruce Wayne wonder what he was thinking or feeling.

Focus BW, he told himself. Bruce Wayne redirected his thoughts back to running as he remembered his mom's words about being distracted by what other people were doing. So, Bruce Wayne refocused and kept his eye towards his target. Unlike his opponent, Bruce Wayne put on a crooked smile on his face as he thought about all the training that he had gotten from Tux. He truly appreciated it.

What?!!.....Bruce Wayne was in shock. About fifty yards from the finish line was the last basket. He hoped that it was a flavor that he did NOT like....

Oohh no!...BISON.....his most favorite! He could smell it immediately. He had to stop.

As he had done before, as soon as he seized the bison cookie with his teeth, he took off like a rocket. It had cost him though because he was seconds behind the stoic dog. But Bruce Wayne didn't care. The deliciousness in his mouth was well worth it, and he was enjoying himself.

Thirty yards from the finish line, he clearly heard his mom shout, "Run Bruce Wayne! You can do it! RUN!!!"

Reassuring words from his mom, and a reminder. Of course I can do it, he told himself. I can have everything I want, I can have everything I want, he repeated to himself as he focused on the finish line. Because he truly believed his words, his legs responded accordingly and ran with so much speed. He felt as if he were flying, and he was to those watching him.

At the last ten yards of the race, Bruce Wayne finally caught up with the stoic Doberman Pincher...... tied the race....and, got everything he wanted.

Printed in the United States
by Baker & Taylor Publisher Services